# THE
# SHERLOCK
# HOLMES

## CHILDREN'S COLLECTION

### MYSTERY, MISCHIEF
### AND MAYHEM

Published by Sweet Cherry Publishing Limited
Unit 36, Vulcan House,
Vulcan Road,
Leicester, LE5 3EF
United Kingdom

First published in the UK in 2020
2020 edition

2 4 6 8 10 9 7 5 3 1

ISBN: 978-1-78226-427-9

Cover design by Arianna Bellucci and Rhiannon Izard
Illustrations by Arianna Bellucci

www.sweetcherrypublishing.com

Printed and bound in China
C.WM004

# SHERLOCK HOLMES

# THE MUSGRAVE RITUAL

## SIR ARTHUR CONAN DOYLE

Sherlock Holmes is a puzzle. His mind is orderly, precise and as sharp as a knife. Yet in other ways he is one of the untidiest people I have ever met. Not that I am particularly tidy myself – and I should be, as a doctor. But Holmes drives me mad!

When we lived together, he kept his cigars in the coal bucket, and

his tobacco in the toe of a Persian
slipper. His unanswered post was
fixed to the wooden mantelpiece
with a knife!

His shooting habits were
not much better. I have always
believed that gun practice should
be done outdoors. Yet Holmes
would happily sit in his armchair,

with a box of bullets by his side,
and cover the walls with the
initials of our dear Queen Victoria.
I do not think that our sitting
room was improved by having
VR written in bullet holes.

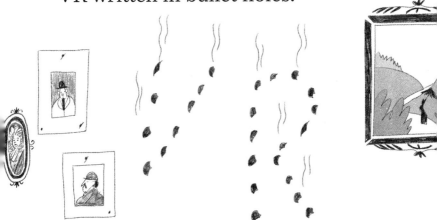

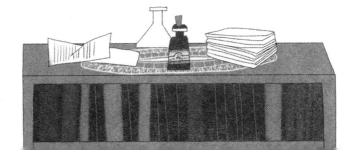

Plus, our rooms were always full of chemicals. They had a funny way of turning up in the butter dish, bathtub, or even worse places. I will never forget the time Mrs Hudson served us tea that, when poured, was fizzing, foaming and bright blue! I don't think she has ever recovered from that shock.

Most of all, Holmes hated to destroy papers. Especially those about past cases. It was only once every year or two that he would bother to sort them out.

Month after month, his paper collection grew, until every corner of the room was stacked with bundles. They could not be burned or put away by anyone except Holmes himself – or so he said.

One winter's night, we were sitting together in front of the fire.

'Holmes,' I said, turning to my friend. 'Why don't you use this evening to do a little tidying up?'

He knew that I was right. So, with a sheepish expression, he went off to his bedroom. He returned after a moment with a large tin box. He put the box in the middle of the floor, kneeled down beside it and pulled off the lid.

I could see that it was already half full of bundles of papers. Each was tied up with red tape.

'There are a lot of cases in here, Watson,' he said, looking at me with a playful grin. 'I think if you knew what I had in this box, you would ask me to pull some out instead of putting others in.'

'These are records of your early work, then?' I asked.

'I have often wished that I had notes of those cases.'

'Yes, my friend, these all happened long before you began writing about my cases.'

Holmes lifted out bundle after bundle of paper.

'They are not all successes, Watson,' he said. 'But there are some interesting problems among them. Here is the record of the Tarleton murders, and the adventure of the old Russian woman. There is also a full account of Ricoletti with the club foot, and his dreadful wife. And here – ah, now, this is something a little unusual.'

Holmes dived his arm down into the piles of papers and brought up a small wooden box with a sliding lid. From inside, he pulled out a crumpled piece of paper. Then came an old-fashioned brass key, a short wooden peg with a ball of string attached to it, and three rusty, metal discs.

'Well, Watson, what do you make of this lot?' he asked, smiling at my expression.

'It's a strange collection,' I replied.

'Very strange, and the story of these things is stranger still.'

'These items have a history, then?' I asked.

'So much so that they are *part of* history,' Holmes said.

'What do you mean by that?'

Holmes picked them up one by one and laid them on the table. Then he sat down in his chair again and looked at them. His eyes shone with satisfaction, as if he were looking at a golden trophy.

'These are all that I have left to remind me of the adventure of the Musgrave Ritual,' he said.

I had heard Holmes mention the Musgrave Ritual before, but he had never told me the details.

'Will you tell me about it?' I asked.

'And leave the room in such a mess?' he asked, mischievously.

16

I smiled.

'I would be glad to tell you about it,' Holmes said. 'You can add the case to your collection. It is certainly different from any other criminal records of this country. Or any other country, for that matter.

'Do you remember me telling you about the affair of the *Gloria Scott?* It was my first case – the kick-start of my career as a detective. Nowadays, my name is known far and wide. The public

and the police force both see
me as the man who can solve
mysteries. But it was not always
like that.'

I settled myself comfortably
to listen to his story. I was trying
very hard to ignore the mess.

'When you first met me,
Watson, I had already made a
name for myself. Although it was
not a name that paid much.

'When I first came to London
I had rooms in Montague Street,

just around the corner from the British Museum. I spent endless hours in there, studying all the branches of science that might make me better at my job.

'Now and again, small cases came my way. They were mainly through old fellow students. The third of these cases was the Musgrave Ritual. It is because of this strange case, and the interest people had in it, that I became the detective I am today.'

We were interrupted by Mrs
Hudson bringing our supper.
Luckily, Holmes continued
speaking as we ate. I think I was
hungrier for the story than I was
for our ham and eggs.

'Reginald Musgrave had been
at the same university as myself,'
Holmes said, 'and I knew him
slightly. He was not very popular
among the other students. They all
thought he was a proud person, but
I believe that he was simply shy.

'He had a very fine appearance with his thin, high nose and his large, bright eyes. He was always very polite. He was part of one of the oldest families in the country. Their manor house, Hurlstone, is perhaps the oldest inhabited building in Sussex. Whenever I saw his

pale, keen face or the elegant way he held his head, I thought of that grand old house. The grey archways and decorative windows swam into my mind.

'Once or twice we talked together. He often seemed very interested in my detective work.'

Holmes and I finished our meal and went back to our chairs by the fire. I couldn't think of a better way to spend a winter's evening. While I stared into the flames, Holmes resumed his tale.

'For four years after university, I saw nothing of Reginald Musgrave. Then, one morning, he walked into my rooms in Montague Street.

He had hardly changed at all. He was dressed very fashionably, and he had the same quiet, smooth manner that I remembered.

'"How have you been, Musgrave?" I asked, shaking his hand.

'"You probably heard about my poor father's death two years ago," he said. "Since then I have had the Hurlstone house to manage. I am also a Member of

Parliament, so my life has been busy. But I understand, Holmes, that you are now using your amazing powers in your work as a detective?"

"'Yes, that's right," I said.

"'I am delighted to hear it," he said, "because I need your advice. We have had some very strange happenings at Hurlstone. It is an odd and baffling business. The police have not been able to explain it."

'You can imagine how excited I was, Watson. I had been waiting months for an interesting case. In my heart I knew that I could succeed where others failed. Now I had the opportunity to test myself.'

Holmes paused. He was too good at keeping me in suspense.

'Give me the details!' I cried, impatiently. I was already leaning forwards in my chair.

Holmes held up a hand and I sat back.

'Reginald Musgrave sat down opposite me in that very chair, Watson. He told me his story.

"'I am not married," Musgrave explained. "But I do have a lot of servants at Hurlstone. It's a big old place and takes a lot of looking after. In the hunting season I usually have a large party, so I need a lot of help to host it. Altogether there are eight maids, the cook, the butler, two footmen, and a boy. The garden and the stables, of course, have separate staff."'

Holmes paused again to look at me and I raised my eyebrows. We were both amazed at the number of staff employed to look after one person.

'Musgrave continued with his story: "Brunton has been with us the longest out of all the staff. He is the butler. He was a young, out-of-work school teacher when he was first taken on by my father.

He is a man of great energy and character, so he soon became vital in the household.

"'Brunton is a tall, handsome man. He cannot be more than forty now. He can speak several languages and plays nearly every musical instrument under the sun. So it's wonderful that he has been happy in a butler position for so long. I suppose he's comfortable. He probably doesn't have the energy to make a change. Everyone who visits us always remembers Brunton, the butler.

'"But this perfect man has one fault, Mr Holmes. He is far too fond of the ladies. You can imagine that for a man like him, it is easy to get the attention of lots of young ladies. Especially since we live in such a quiet country district, with few other handsome, talented men. When he was married he was all right, but since his wife died we have had a lot of trouble with him.

"'A few months ago, we hoped that he may settle down again. He had asked Rachel Howells, our second housemaid, to marry him. But it did not last. He finished with her and started a new relationship with Janet Tregellis.

She is the daughter of the head gamekeeper.

"'Rachel is a very good girl but is very excitable. Brunton broke her heart. She goes about the house now – or did until yesterday – like a shadow of her former self. She is always miserable.

"'That was our first drama at Hurlstone, but a second one came that was far more horrible. We had to sack Brunton becuase of it. He is an intelligent man and is curious about everything – even things that do not concern him. I had no idea how serious this habit was until recently.

"'Last Thursday night I could not sleep. I had made the mistake of drinking a cup of strong black coffee after my dinner. At two o'clock in the morning, I finally gave up hope – sleeping was impossible. I got up and lit a candle, hoping that a little reading might help me drift off to sleep. I had left my book in the sitting room so I put on my dressing gown and went to get it.

"'As I looked down the corridor, I was surprised to see a glimmer of light. It was coming from the open door of the library. Yet I had put out the lamp myself and closed the door before going to bed.

"'I first thought that it was burglars. Luckily, the corridors of Hurlstone are decorated with old weapons. I put down my candle and took a battleaxe off the wall. Then I crept on tiptoe down the corridor and peeped in at the open door.

36

"'Brunton was in the library. He was sitting in a chair with a piece of paper that looked like a map laid out over his knees. His forehead was resting in one hand and his eyes were narrowed, as if he was deep in thought.

"'I stood there, silently, watching Brunton from the darkness. A small candle on the edge of the table gave out just enough light to show me that, strangely, he was still fully dressed.

'"Suddenly, as I watched, Brunton got up from his chair and walked over to the desk. He unlocked it and opened one of the drawers. He took out a paper, went back to his seat, and flattened it out beside the candle. Then he began to study it closely.

'"I was very angry now. He was looking at our private family documents as if he were casually reading the newspaper! I stepped forwards. Brunton looked up and

saw me standing in the doorway.
He sprang to his feet, looking
frightened and clasping the paper
to his chest.

"'So,' I said. 'This is how you repay the trust we have shown you. You will leave my service tomorrow!'

"'Brunton bowed, dropped the paper and slunk past me without a word. By the candlelight, I managed to read what was written on the paper. Oddly, it was nothing important at all. It was just a copy of the questions and answers for the Musgrave Ritual. It's a strange old family custom.'"

Holmes paused in his telling of Musgrave's story. He must have seen how interested I was, because he gave a small smile and his eyes twinkled. Holmes loved an audience, even if it was just me, and he knew how to tell a good story.

'The Musgrave Ritual,' I said. 'Do continue, Holmes.'

'Reginald Musgrave told me that it was a sort of ceremony. Each Musgrave, for centuries past, has gone through it when they reached twenty-one. Only the family itself, and perhaps a few historians, would have been interested in it. It had no practical use whatever.'

'"We'd better talk more about this paper after you have finished your story," I said to Musgrave.

'"If you think it is really necessary," he answered, looking a little confused.

'"I relocked the desk using the key that Brunton had

left," Musgrave continued. "I had just turned to go when I was surprised to find that Brunton had come back. He was standing in front of me.

"'Mr Musgrave, sir,' he cried. His voice was husky with emotion. 'I cannot bear the shame, sir. I have always been proud of my job here. The disgrace of leaving it would kill me. My blood will be on your head, sir, if you throw me out.

If you really must fire me, then do not do it yet. Let me work for one more month. After that, I can pretend that I quit the job. I could stand that. But not to be thrown out in front of all the staff – the people that I know so well.'

""You don't deserve it, Brunton,' I answered. 'Your behaviour has been disgraceful. You have worked for my family for a long time, so I don't want to embarrass you in front of the staff. But a month is too long. Leave in a week, and give whatever reason you like for going.'

""'Only a week, sir!' he cried, in a tear-filled voice. 'Two weeks, say at least two weeks!'

""'A week,' I repeated. 'And you don't deserve even that.'

"'He crept away, his face sunk on his chest like a broken man. I put out the light and went back to my room.

"'For two days after this, Brunton did his work well. I did not

45

mention what had happened. I just waited curiously to see how he would explain it to the rest of the staff. On the third morning, however, he did not come to me after breakfast. He always comes to me after breakfast, to get my instructions for the day.

"'As I left the dining room, I happened to meet Rachel Howells, the maid. I have told you how upset and ill she had been. She looked so awfully pale this time, that I told her off for being at work.

""You should be in bed,' I said. 'Come back to work when you are stronger.'

"'She looked at me with such a strange expression.

""I am strong enough, Mr Musgrave,' she said.

""'Well, we will see what the doctor says,' I answered. 'You must stop work now. When you go downstairs, please tell Brunton that I want to see him.'

""'The butler has gone,' she said.

""'Gone! Gone where?' I asked.

""'He is gone. No one has seen him. He is not in his room. Oh, yes, he is gone, he is gone!'

"'She fell back against the wall with a shriek of laughter. I was

48

horrified at her sudden change of mood – she seemed almost insane. I rushed to ring the bell for help. The girl was taken to her room, screaming and sobbing. I asked the other staff about Brunton.

"'He had certainly disappeared. His bed had not been slept

in and he had not been seen by anyone since he went to his room the night before. It was difficult to see how he could have left the house. The windows and doors were all still locked in the morning. His clothes, his watch, and even his money were in his room, but the black suit that he usually wore was missing. His slippers, too, were gone, but his boots were left behind. Where could Brunton have gone in the night, and what could have happened to him?

"'As I have said, Hurlstone is a huge house. The old wing, which is now hardly used, is particularly large. But we searched the whole place, from cellar to attic. There was no trace of him. I could not believe that he would leave without taking any of his things. Where could he be?

"'I called the local police, but they have not been able to help.

Rain had fallen the night before, so there were no footprints or other clues on the lawn or paths around the house.

"'Then something even *more* dramatic happened!

"'For two days, Rachel Howells had been so ill that a nurse had been brought in to sit with her at night. On the third night after Brunton's disappearance, Rachel was sleeping so well that the nurse had a nap in the armchair.

When the nurse awoke in the early morning, Rachel was gone. Her bed was empty, the window was open, and there was no sign of her.

"'The staff woke me up. I went with two servants in search of the missing girl. It was not difficult to follow her trail. Starting from under her window, there was a series of small footprints crossing the lawn. When we got to the edge of the lake, the footprints suddenly disappeared.

'"The lake is very deep. You can imagine how worried we were when we saw that the girl's trail stopped at the edge of it.

'"We searched the lake at once. But there was no trace of a body. We did find something else though – something very odd indeed. It was a linen bag, full of old, rusted metal and dull-coloured pieces of pebble and glass. We still don't know what happened to either Rachel Howells or Richard Brunton. The county police are at their wits' end. So I have come to you, Holmes."'

The fire had grown smaller and I felt a slight chill prickling my arms. I reached for the tongs to put some more coal on the fire. Holmes took a sip of

his after-dinner coffee and continued talking.

'You can imagine, Watson, how interested I was by this strange chain of events. I tried to piece them together. The butler was gone, the maid was gone. The maid had loved the butler, but he broke her heart and then she hated him. She was fiery and passionate. She had been terribly nervous right after Brunton's disappearance. She had flung a bag full of very strange items into the lake. These were all things to think about, but there was still something missing. What was the first event in this chain?

"'I must see the paper," I said to Musgrave. "The one that this butler of yours risked losing his job over."

"'This Ritual of ours is a rather stupid thing," Reginald Musgrave said. "But it is very old and has

become a family tradition. I have a
copy of the questions and answers
here if you want to look at them."

'He handed me the very paper
that I have here, Watson. This
is the strange riddle that each
Musgrave man must try to solve,
although no one has ever
succeeded.
I will read you
the questions
and answers
just as they are.'

Whose was it?

His who is gone.

Who shall have it?

He who will come.

Where was the sun?

Over the oak.

Where was the shadow?

Under the elm.

How was it stepped?

North by ten, east by five, south by two, west by one, and so under.

What shall we give for it?

All that is ours.

Why should we give it?

For the sake of the trust.

Holmes handed me the paper. I silently read it through again, trying to make more sense of it.

'Musgrave told me that the original had no date on it,' went on Holmes. 'But it's written in the spelling of the middle of the seventeenth century. It is a very old tradition, indeed. Musgrave didn't think it would help in solving the case. But I did.

'"It gives us another mystery," I said to Musgrave. "And one that is even more interesting than the first. It may be that the solution of one mystery could give us the solution of the other. You will excuse me saying this, Musgrave, but your butler seems to be a very clever man. More clever than ten generations of his employers."

""I don't quite understand," said Musgrave. "The paper seems to me to be of no real importance."

""To me it seems very important," I said. "I'm sure that

Brunton thought the same. He had probably seen the paper before the night you caught him reading it."

"'It's very possible," replied Musgrave. "We never tried to hide it."

"'He just wanted to remind himself of the answers, I imagine. You say that he had some sort of map or chart laid out? He was comparing it to the answers on the paper, I believe."

'"That is true. But what could Brunton have to do with this old family custom of ours? What does this nonsense mean?"

'"Oh, it will not be very hard to find out," I told Musgrave. "I think we should take the first train down to Sussex. We shall solve the mystery in no time."

'That same afternoon, we went to Hurlstone. The famous old building is in the shape of an L. The longer side of the L is the more modern section, and the shorter side is the old part. The date 1607 is carved over the door, but experts agree that the building is much, much older than that. The thick walls and tiny windows of the old part made it a very uncomfortable place to live. So the family built the new, more modern wing in the last century. The old one was then used as a storehouse and cellar.

'A beautiful park, full of very old trees, surrounds the house. The lake is close, too. It's a truly lovely place.

'I was already sure, Watson, that all of the mysteries were connected. I knew that if I could read the Musgrave Ritual, I would hold in my hand the most important clue. A clue that would lead me to the truth about Brunton the butler, and Howells, the heart-broken maid.'

'I can see that, Holmes,' I agreed. 'This Ritual seems to be at the centre of it all.'

'Exactly, Watson. Why should the butler be so keen to solve this old riddle? He must have seen something in it that all the generations of Reginald Musgrave's family had missed. Money, that's what, Watson. It must have been something valuable. What exactly was it then? And how did it lead to Brunton's disappearance?

'I knew that the measurements in the Ritual must refer to some spot on the property. If we could find that spot, we would be part way to finding what the secret was. It must be an important secret for the Musgrave family to hide it in such a strange way. There were two trees mentioned in the Ritual that could give us a clue: an oak and an elm. The oak tree was plain to see. It was right in front of the house, on the left-hand side of the drive. It was huge! It was one of the most magnificent trees that I have ever seen.'

'"Was the oak tree alive when the Ritual was written?" I asked Musgrave, as we drove past it.

'"Yes. It has probably been there since the Norman conquest in the eleventh century," he answered. "The distance around its trunk is equal to four tall men, laid end to end."

"'Are there any old elm trees in the garden?" I asked.

"'There used to be a very old one over there, but it was struck by lightning ten years ago. We had to cut it down."

"'Can you see where it used to be?" I asked.

"'Oh, yes, the stump is still there."

"'Are there any other elms?"

'"No old ones, but plenty of beech trees."

'"I see. I would like to see where the old elm tree grew."

'We had driven up in a dog-cart. Reginald Musgrave led me away to the place where the elm tree had once stood. It was nearly halfway between the oak tree

### Dog-cart

Simple wooden carts drawn by one horse and used on country estates. Some have one seat for the driver and passenger. Some have back-to-back seats. Have a tendency to throw mud onto the left side. Originally, rear seat folded down to accommodate dogs, hence the name.

and the house. My investigation seemed to be moving on nicely.

"'I suppose it is impossible to find out how tall the elm tree was?" I asked Musgrave.

"'I can tell you at once," he replied. "It was sixty-four feet high."

"'How do you know that?" I asked in surprise.

"'When my old tutor used to give me an exercise in maths, it was often about measuring heights. When I was a boy, I worked out the height of every tree and building on the estate."

'This was an unexpected piece of luck, Watson.

'"Did your butler ever ask the same question?" I asked Musgrave.

'Musgrave looked at me in astonishment. "Yes, he did! He asked about the height of the elm tree some months ago. He said he'd had a little argument with the groom about it."

'This was excellent news, Watson. It showed me that I was on the right track. I looked up at the sun. It was low in the sky. In less than an hour it would lie just over the branches of the old oak – as it said in the Ritual. At exactly that time, I had to find where the end of the elm tree's shadow would have fallen,' Sherlock explained.

'That must have been difficult, Holmes, when the elm was no longer there,' I said.

'Well, I knew that if Brunton could do it, I could do it too. I went with Musgrave to his study and took a small wooden peg, a long piece of string and two tall fishing rods. Using these, and a few easy calculations, I was able to work out where the tree's shadow would have ended.

The end of the shadow would have almost hit the wall of the house. I put the wooden peg in the ground at that spot. You can imagine my triumph, Watson, when I saw a dip in the ground right near my peg. I knew that it was the mark Brunton the butler made when he worked out these same measurements himself. I was still on his trail.

'I then looked at my compass and began to walk. Ten steps to the north, just as the Ritual said. This took me further along the side of the house. Again, I marked my spot with a peg. Then I took five steps to the east and two steps to the south. It brought me to an old door. I opened it and took one step to the west. It took me to a stone-floored passage. This was the place the Ritual's riddle was leading to.

'I have never felt such a cold chill of disappointment, Watson. For a moment, I thought that there must be a big mistake in my maths. The setting sun shone through the open door. I could see that the old, grey floor stones were firmly cemented together. They had not been moved for many years. Brunton had not been at work here. I tapped on the floor, but it sounded the same all over, and there was no sign of any crack or gap.

'Luckily, though, Musgrave was following my lead. He took out his copy of the Ritual.

"'And under!" he cried. "Holmes, you are not wrong. You have just missed out the 'and under'."

'I had thought at first, Watson, that it meant that we were to dig.

But I saw that I was wrong. "Is there a cellar under here, then?" I cried.

'"Yes, there is! And it is as old as the house. It is down here, through this door," Musgrave replied.

'We walked down the winding stone stairs.

Musgrave struck a match and lit a large lantern that stood on a barrel in the corner. In an instant, we knew that we had found the right place. It was clear, however, that we had not been the only people to visit this cellar.

'It had been used for storing wood, but the logs had been pushed to the sides to leave a space in the middle. In this space was a large, heavy, rectangular stone, with a rusted iron ring in

the centre. Attached to it was a
thick, checked scarf.

'"By Jove!" cried my client.
"That's Brunton's scarf. I could
swear to it. What has the villain
been doing here?"

'I asked Musgrave to call the
police. Then I tried to lift the

stone by pulling on the scarf. I
could only move it slightly – it was
amazingly heavy. It was
only with the help of
a policeman that
I could move
the stone to
one side.

We all peered into the black hole beneath us. Musgrave knelt down and lowered the lantern into the hole.

'We saw that it was a very small room. At one side of the room was a wooden box, covered with dull brass strips. The lid was open and a strange, old-fashioned key was sticking out of the lock. There was a thick layer of dust on the outside. Damp and worms had eaten through the wood, and a small group of mushrooms was growing on the inside of the box. A collection of old coins, like the ones I have here, were scattered over the bottom of the box. There was nothing else. Only mould, mushrooms and old coins.

'But, at that moment, I could not concentrate on the wooden box. My eyes were fixed on the man beside it – the dead man. He was kneeling down with his head pressed onto the edge of the box

and his hands tightly gripping either side of it. He was dressed in a black suit. From his height, his clothes and his hair, Musgrave could tell that it was Brunton, his missing butler.

'He had been dead for some days, but there were no wounds or bruises to show how he had died. Once his body had been carried from the cellar, we realised that we still had a problem. A problem that was almost as difficult as the one that we had at the start.

'I admit that so far, Watson, I had been disappointed in my investigation. I thought I would solve the case as soon as I found the Ritual's secret hiding place. Even though I had now found it, I still had no idea what the hidden treasure was. It's true that I had discovered that Brunton had died. But now I had to work out *how* he had died, and what the maid had to do with this horrible plot. I sat down in the corner of the room and thought the whole matter over carefully.

'You know my methods in such cases, Watson. I put myself in the man's place and tried to imagine what I would do in the same situation. In this case, the matter was made easier by Brunton's high intelligence. I was pleased that I didn't have to imagine it through a less clever brain than my own. It is so tiresome when I have to do that.

'Brunton knew that something valuable was hidden. He had discovered the hiding place. He found that the stone that covered it was too heavy for a man to move on his own. What would he do next? He could not get help from outside. It was better to have help from inside the house, from someone he knew. But whom could he ask? Rachel

Howells, of course. The maid had loved him, after all. Brunton probably believed that she *still* loved him, even though he treated her horribly. The butler would try to make peace with Miss Howells, and then would ask for her help. Together, they would come to the cellar in the middle of the night. Together, they would be strong enough to lift the stone. So far, I could follow their actions as if I had actually seen them.

'But the stone was incredibly heavy. The burly policeman and I found it tricky enough to move. It would have been even more difficult for Brunton and Miss Howells. I wondered what they could have done to make it easier. I carefully looked at all the pieces of wood that were scattered around the cellar floor. Some of them were flattened at the sides and another had a deep dent at one end. Of course! They must have moved the stone just slightly and pushed pieces of wood into the gap. The more wood they pushed into the gap, the more it raised the heavy stone. As soon as there was a space big enough to crawl through, they propped

the stone up with one piece of wood and crawled into the hole. So far it was all making sense to me.'

Holmes fixed me with his dark stare and sipped his coffee again. He was enjoying keeping me in suspense. But I waited patiently for the next part of the story, trying hard not to show how desperate I was to hear it.

'But the question is: what happened next?' Holmes continued, after putting down his

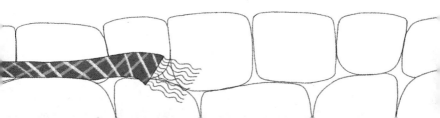

coffee. 'Clearly, only one person could fit into the hole at a time. So Brunton crawled through, while the maid waited above. Brunton then unlocked the box, handed up whatever treasures were inside and then … and then what?

'Was the girl still angry at Brunton for treating her badly? Did she see her chance of revenge? Or was it by accident that the wood had slipped and the stone had slammed shut – trapping

Brunton in the hole? Had the maid's only crime been to stay silent instead of going for help? Or had she kicked away the wood and laughed as the stone slab crashed down on top of Brunton?

'I can imagine Miss Howells,

clutching at her treasure trove and running wildly up the winding stairs. I can see her smile widening as she listened to the muffled screams behind her. Enjoying the sound of desperate hands drumming against the slab of stone.

'If she was guilty, it would explain her pale face and shaken nerves the next morning. But what had been in the box? And what had she done with it? Then it came to me – the box must have been filled with the old metal and pebbles that Musgrave found in the lake. Miss Howells had probably thrown them in there so no one would discover that she had committed the crime.

'For twenty minutes I sat quite still, thinking the matter out. Though I know that does not interest you, Watson. When you write this story down, it will be

all fistfights and action, I'm sure.'
Holmes chuckled.

I was about to say something,
when I saw the grin stretch across
Holmes' face. He often liked to
tease me about my writing. I
smiled back and waited for him to
continue.

'While I was putting the facts
together in my head, Musgrave
was stuck to the spot. He was
standing above the hole, swinging
his lantern and peering down into

the darkness. His face was pale from shock.

"'These are coins of King Charles I," he said. He held out the few that had been in the box. "You see, we were right at dating the Ritual back to the seventeenth century."

'"We may find something else of Charles I," I said. The meaning of the first two questions in the Ritual had suddenly come to me. "Let me see the contents of the bag that you fished out of the lake."

'We went up to Musgrave's study, and he laid the things in front of me. I could understand why he would think they were unimportant. They looked like junk. The metal was almost black and the stones were very dull.

I rubbed one of them on my sleeve and it glowed like a spark. It was clear that the jagged metal had once been a perfect circle, but it had been bent out of shape.

'I said, "You must remember that after the death of King Charles I, the royal family fled. They probably left many of their most precious things buried behind in England. They would have planned to come back for them after the civil war."

'"My ancestor, Sir Ralph Musgrave, fled with King Charles II to Europe," said Reginald Musgrave.

'"Well now!" I said. "I think that should give us the last link to our chain. Despite the sad events that led us here, I must congratulate you for owning such a precious antique. It is a historical treasure."

'"What is it then?" asked Reginald Musgrave.

'"It is nothing less than the ancient crown of the kings of England."

I looked at Holmes in astonishment and he smiled.

'Yes,' he nodded. 'That is the look that Musgrave had too.

'"The crown!" cried Musgrave.

'"Precisely," I said. "Remember

what the Ritual says: 'Whose was it? He who is gone.' That was after the death of Charles I. Then, 'Who shall have it? He who will come.' That was his son, Charles II. I am very sure that this battered and shapeless piece of metal once sat on the heads of the royal Stuart family."

"'How did it come to be in the lake?" asked Musgrave.

"'Ah, that's a question that will take some time to answer."

'I explained to him, Watson, the whole long chain of events that I had put together. Before my story was even finished, the sky had folded into darkness and the moon was brightly shining.

'"And how was it that Charles II did not fetch this crown when he came back to England?" asked Musgrave, pushing the antique back into its linen bag.

'"That's the one answer we will probably never know. Perhaps the

Musgrave man who had hidden the crown here died before Charles returned. He left the Ritual to the next generations of his family without ever explaining the meaning of it. From that day on, it was handed down from father to son. Then, at last, it came within reach of a man who uncovered its secret. But he lost his life in the process.'"

Holmes gazed at the Ritual for a moment and then looked at me.

'There we have it, Watson. That is the story of the Musgrave Ritual. They have kept the crown at Hurlstone, you know. I'm sure that if you mentioned my name, they would be happy to show it to you.'

I planned to do just that. I would very much enjoy seeing such a special piece of history.

'And what about the maid, Miss Howells?' I asked.

Holmes shrugged.

'No one ever found her. She probably left the country. She may have taken herself and the memory of her crime to some land beyond the seas.'

The clock chimed midnight and I got up to go to bed. I smiled as I looked around. The room was even messier than when Holmes started his story. But at least it had been an interesting evening.

# Sherlock Holmes

World-renowned private detective Sherlock Holmes has solved hundreds of mysteries, and is the author of such fascinating monographs as *Early English Charters* and *The Influence of a Trade Upon the Form of a Hand*. He keeps bees in his free time.

# Dr John Watson

Wounded in action at Maiwand, Dr John Watson left the army and moved into 221B Baker Street. There he was surprised to learn that his new friend, Sherlock Holmes, faced daily peril solving crimes, and began documenting his investigations. Dr Watson also runs a doctor's practice.